ANIMAL
S.O.S.

THE HIDDEN
PUPPY RESCUE

To Chloe and Gabby, with love. And with a
great big thank you to Laura Head – KM
To my grandma, with lots of love, Katy – KJ

STRIPES PUBLISHING
An imprint of Little Tiger Press
1 The Coda Centre, 189 Munster Road,
London SW6 6AW

A paperback original
First published in Great Britain in 2013

Text copyright © Kelly McKain, 2013
Illustrations copyright © Katy Jackson, 2013

ISBN: 978-1-84715-256-5

ANIMAL S.O.S.

THE HIDDEN PUPPY RESCUE

KELLY McKAIN
Illustrated by Katy Jackson

MAP OF WHITE HORSE BAY

Vet's

Cliff-top Path

High Cliffs

Café

Beach

NOT TO SCALE

Harbour Lane

Harbour Lane

East Reach
House B&B

This way
to Rescue
Centre

Newsagent's

This way to
White Horse Stables

Harbour

CHAPTER ONE

"Oh, he's gorgeous!" Amy cried, gazing at Carrie's photo of the cute Labrador puppy.

"He makes Rufus look huge!" Leah exclaimed, as her big shaggy dog bounced around beside them.

"He's called Oscar," Carrie told them. "I've only had him a week."

Amy and Leah were in the yard at White Horse Stables. Carrie had just started riding there and she and the rest of her group were back from their lesson, so the girls were helping them all to dismount and

7

untack. Amy and Leah often gave Jane the
stable girl a hand with the chores and
getting the ponies ready to ride. There were
all the usual Saturday lessons going on, as
well as a group of tourists arriving for a
hack out with Dan, Leah's dad, and
George, her older brother, as they did every
day in the summer holidays. The yard was
busy, buzzing with people and ponies, and
Amy couldn't think of anywhere
she'd rather spend a sunny
afternoon.

Amy held on to Carrie's pony's bridle while she ran up her stirrups. "Why don't you come round and see Oscar sometime?" Carrie suggested.

"Really?" said Amy. "Oh, I'd love to!"

"Yeah, of course," said Carrie, "and you, too, Leah."

Leah smiled. "That would be nice. If I can ever get away from this place."

"Oh, here's Mum now," said Carrie, waving towards a blue sports car that had just pulled into the car park. "I'll go and check if it's OK."

A few minutes later, she hurried back and invited Amy and Leah to come round at two o'clock the next day.

"Great!" cried Amy. "See you then!" She waved to Carrie and the other girls as they made their way over to the car park. Then she turned to Leah, expecting her to look just as excited, but Leah was frowning.

"Surely if we explain to your mum about Oscar, she'll give you a couple of hours off," Amy said.

"No, it's not that," Leah replied. "It's just, I thought he looked a bit small to be away from his mother. Still, it's hard to tell from a picture."

"Maybe he was the runt of the litter," Amy suggested.

Leah shrugged. "Yeah, probably."

Just then, Jane came up, clipboard in hand. "Hi, girls. How did you get on with my list?" she asked them.

"We tacked up Barney and Petal, and Prince is just in from a lesson, so we've given him a drink and loosened his girth while he's waiting," Leah reported.

"And Bella and Guinevere are in from the field and brushed down, but we haven't got their tack on yet," Amy added. "I think that was all of them, wasn't it?"

Jane smiled. "I'm impressed. You'd make a great stable girl, Amy," she said.

Amy couldn't help grinning. It wasn't so long ago – just in the Easter holidays, in fact – that she'd had her first riding lesson. Now she felt totally at home on the yard, and pretty confident handling the ponies. Rosie said her riding was really coming on, too – she could canter now, and she was hoping to have a go at jumping soon as well.

They all looked round as a minibus pulled into the car park. "Oh, here are the tourists," said Leah. "Come on, Amy – if we're quick we can finish getting Bella and Guinny ready while Mum's sorting the riders out with hats and boots."

"Thanks, girls," said Jane. Then she glanced at her watch. "And don't forget your own lesson, Amy. It's nearly half two now. As soon as we get this group mounted up and away, Leah's mum will be ready for you."

"Wow, time flies when you're having fun!" cried Amy with a grin.

"When you're run off your feet, you mean!" grumbled Leah, but she was smiling, too.

Amy and Leah finished getting the tourists' horses and ponies ready. Then they headed over to the tack room to grab a lead rope for Gracie, the lovely sweet-natured grey pony that Amy always rode. Amy couldn't wait to go and get her in from the field. They'd been far too busy all day to even go up and say hello to her, or to Leah's pony, Nutmeg. Just as they were crossing the yard Leah's mum, Rosie, came out of the office.

"Hey, Mum, is it all right if I ride Nutmeg in the second manège while Amy has her lesson?" Leah asked. "I'm not going to see him all day otherwise."

Rosie frowned. "Usually you could, but I've already told Billy he can lunge Spark in there while the yard's quiet."

"Oh, OK," said Leah. Amy could see how disappointed she was and she had a sudden thought. "Could Leah ride in with me?" she asked. "I loved riding with her and Billy when we were working with Spark."

Leah grinned at her. "Yeah, could I?" she asked Rosie. "It would do Nutmeg good to have a lesson – go over the basics."

"Yes, all right," said Rosie, "so long as you two promise not to distract each other!"

"As if we would!" giggled Leah.

The girls went and grabbed two lead ropes before hurrying off to get Nutmeg and Gracie in from the field. On the way they met Billy coming down the track with Spark. Billy hadn't been coming to the yard long, but already he felt like part of the furniture. The sleek black pony walked calmly by his side, with the lead rope slack between them. It was hard to imagine that

ANIMAL S.O.S.

Spark had been that distressed, bewildered animal they'd found running loose on the road only a couple of weeks ago – the same one they'd helped Billy to bring to White Horse Stables, and launched an Animal S.O.S. mission to help keep him! Thinking about it made Amy wonder if she and Leah would have any more exciting adventures over the summer.

"Hi, Billy!" she said brightly. "How's it going?" She walked slowly up to Spark and gave him a gentle pat on the neck.

"Yeah, really well, thanks," said Billy. "He's so much more relaxed already."

"That's great," said Amy.

"We'll have to all go out on a hack together again soon," said Leah. "I'll ask Mum when she might be free to take us."

"That'd be good," said Billy. "Maybe we could ride on the beach this time. I want to keep giving Spark new challenges."

Amy felt a shiver of excitement rush through her. Riding out on the beach with her friends sounded amazing! She found it hard to believe how much her life had changed in the past three months. There was the move down from London with Mum, opening up the B&B (and working hard to help Mum keep it running smoothly), learning to ride, starting at her new school, and now, in the summer holidays, hanging out at the stables with Leah. Sometimes she felt like she had to pinch herself – it just didn't seem real!

The girls said goodbye to Billy and Spark and hurried up to the field. They got their ponies in, then brushed them down and tacked up as quickly as they could. When they got to the manège, they found that Rosie had laid some trotting poles down on the woodchips. "We're going to have a go at jumping today," she told them, as they walked their ponies round on the track to warm up. Amy felt that shiver of excitement again – jumping!

Rosie explained that they would go over the poles on the ground at first, to help them get their ponies to take nice even strides. When they'd done that, she put up a small cross pole. Leah popped over it as though it wasn't even there, of course, but when it was Amy's turn, she felt her mouth going dry and heard her heart pounding in her ears. She trotted halfway up the short side of the manège, as Leah had done, then turned Gracie off the track to face the jump. One – two – three strides and then – hup, they were over!

"Wow! That was amazing!" gasped Amy, coming to a halt and leaning forward to give Gracie a pat.

"Well done!" cried Leah, "your first jump!"

Rosie was smiling, too. "Right, let's have a couple more goes over this, and then I'll put it up a bit," she said.

Rosie ended up raising the jump twice, in fact, because she said that Amy was doing so well. Both girls got the giggles when Leah knocked a pole down because she was busy chatting, but a stern look from Rosie soon got them back on track. At the end of the lesson, as they walked their ponies round to cool off, feet swinging out of the stirrups, Leah's little brother Adam appeared by the fence. "Back in the beginners' group, are you?" he called to his sister. "That figures!"

"It's always good to brush up on your skills, idiot!" Leah answered back. Amy

18

scowled. Even *she* found Adam annoying.

Once the girls had untacked and turned out their ponies, it was time for Amy's mum to collect her. Leah walked her to the car park and Amy made a big fuss of Rufus before getting in the car.

"See you tomorrow," she called out of the window. "I can't wait to see Oscar!"

"Neither can I!" Leah called back. "See you there!"

"Who's Oscar?" Mum asked Amy later, over pizza and salad back at the B&B. "Not a boy, I hope!"

Amy giggled. "No, he's a puppy!" she told her. Then she explained about Oscar and Carrie. "Leah and I have been invited to visit him tomorrow," she finished. "If that's OK with you, of course. I mean, I'll be here to help with the guests and chores all morning."

Mum glanced at her, and smiled. "Of course it's OK, darling," she said. "I want you to have a good summer, not just be stuck indoors cooking and cleaning all the time."

"I don't mind," Amy insisted. "I know how hard you're working to get the business off the ground." It was great that the B&B was fully booked, but it did mean that most days Mum was on her feet from six in the morning until she went to bed.

"Thanks, love," said Mum. "As soon as we've had this I'm going to set up the breakfast things for the morning, ring a couple of people back about their bookings and then have a bath and go straight to bed. Everyone's here on holiday relaxing and I'm working harder than I've ever done in my life!" But she was smiling as she said it. "It's worth it, though," she added. "Our own business, by the sea! I've already started to get thank-you cards from some of our first guests – that definitely keeps me going, knowing that people have enjoyed themselves. I feel like I've really settled into our new life here," she said. "I hope you have too, darling. I mean, you seem happy, but I know it's a long way from your dad…"

"I do miss him," said Amy, "but we're going on holiday together for a whole week soon, and I know he has me to stay every chance he gets. And I love being here in White Horse Bay."

Mum grinned. "You're turning into quite a country girl," she said, pointing out a big mud splat on Amy's top.

Amy smiled. "It's great being on the yard with my friends, and Gracie and the other ponies. And Rufus, of course." Speaking of Leah's big, shaggy dog made her think about Oscar again. "Oh, Carrie's so lucky to have a new puppy!" she said, with a sigh.

Mum frowned. "Is that a hint? Amy, you know I'm far too busy and exhausted for a dog, and seriously, think about it, you're not here in the week during term time and at the weekends you're often at your dad's..."

"Calm down, Mum!" Amy cried. "I wasn't hinting. Well, maybe I was, but I know it's not practical for us to get one at the moment. Honestly, I do."

"Good," said Mum, "so long as that's clear."

But as she reached for the last slice of pizza, Amy thought to herself that while she really *did* understand why they couldn't have a dog, it didn't stop her desperately wanting one.

CHAPTER TWO

The next afternoon, Amy and Leah met in
the village and went up to Carrie's house.

Leah propped her bike against the
garden wall and Amy virtually dragged her
up the driveway. "Oh, I can't wait to cuddle
little Oscar!" she cried, as she rang the bell.

After a few minutes, when no one had
come to the door, she rang it again. When
there was still no answer, she gave Leah a
puzzled glance. "It was today, wasn't it?" she
asked her.

"Yes," said Leah, "and I know it's the

right house. I came to drop Carrie's school bag back once with Mum, when she'd left it in the office."

"Well, it looks like something must have come up," said Amy. "Come on, let's go—"

But just then, the door swung open and there stood Carrie. Amy saw straight away that she'd been crying. "Oh, Amy, Leah!" she gasped. "I'd forgotten you were coming. Poor Oscar's really ill and we don't know what to do!"

Carrie's mum appeared in the doorway behind her, looking just as upset as her daughter. "Sorry, girls, it's not a great time," she said. "We'll have to—"

But before she could finish, Leah hurried inside, pulling Amy behind her. She rushed into the kitchen, making for a cardboard box on the table. The girls looked in and gasped in shock. Poor Oscar was lying on a blanket, shivering, and his eyes were closed.

He'd been sick and as they watched, he pooed everywhere. The smell was awful. Carrie's mum rushed in and picked him up. "Oh, he's had another bout of diarrhoea, the poor little love," she cried, picking him up and cuddling him close.

Oscar just lay limply in her arms. "Carrie, run and get a towel from the airing cupboard, would you?" she said. "That was the last blanket."

"How long has this been going on?" asked Leah, looking anxiously at Oscar.

"He was sick a couple of hours ago," said Carrie's mum. "We thought that maybe he'd eaten something off the floor. Something he shouldn't have done. But it's got a lot worse now, and I think he's got a temperature."

She grabbed some kitchen roll, wet it and began to gently clean Oscar up.

"Shall I hold him while you do that?" Amy offered.

"Yes, please," said Carrie's mum.

Amy sat down and took the puppy in her arms. He felt very hot, and he didn't sniff or lick her at all, but just lay still, his breathing fast and shallow. It was clear that something was seriously wrong with him.

"You need to get him to the vet's, right now," said Leah, just as Carrie came back in with the clean towel.

"We haven't even registered him with them yet. We've only just got him," said Carrie's mum, looking anxious. "Oh, I do hope they'll take him!"

"Don't worry," said Leah. "My cousin Kate works there. I'll call her and explain that it's an emergency. Can I borrow your phone, Amy?"

Amy pulled her phone from her trouser pocket and handed it to Leah. Leah spoke to Kate for just a few moments, then hung up. "Mr Ellis can see you in twenty minutes," she told Carrie and her mum. "Kate said to take some spare towels with you and some bags to put the dirty ones in, and wash your hands really well every time you clean him up. If this is a virus, you risk spreading it otherwise."

"Thanks, Leah," said Carrie, giving her a shaky smile. Carrie's mum took Oscar gently from Amy, and placed him back in the cardboard box. Carrie hurried back upstairs for more towels and her mum began rummaging in a drawer for some plastic bags.

"I was just wondering," said Leah. "How old is Oscar? He does seem very small for eight weeks."

"I don't know," said Carrie's mum. "Oh,

28

gosh, do you think he's too young to be away from his mother? We've never had a dog before. We just assumed he was the right age. Carrie's dad bought him as a surprise for her birthday."

Amy saw Leah wince at this, then she asked, "Did he see Oscar with his mum and litter mates? Your husband, I mean, when he went to collect him. And do you have Oscar's papers?"

Carrie's mum looked bewildered. "We don't have any papers. I didn't know we needed any. And no, Jim didn't see the mother. He spotted an ad for the puppies in our local paper and it turned out the breeder was all the way down in Portho, but he offered to meet Jim at that garage by the main road, to save him the journey..." She trailed off and her face fell. "Oh, we should have insisted on seeing the mother, shouldn't we? I didn't think..."

"Yes, you probably should—" Leah began crossly, but Amy caught her eye and gave her a sharp look, to remind her how upset Carrie and her mum already were. Leah swallowed hard. "I'm sure everything will be OK," she managed to say.

Amy held the box with Oscar in while Carrie got in the car, and then she placed it gently on her lap. "Good luck," she said.

Then she shut the door and they drove away.

As the girls watched the car disappear round the corner, Amy frowned at Leah. "You don't think it'll be OK, do you?" she said.

"I hope it will, but… That puppy looked really, really ill to me," Leah said in a near-whisper. "And he's very young to try and fight off such a nasty illness."

"Those questions you were asking – what was that all about?" Amy asked.

Leah sighed. "What Carrie's mum said about meeting the breeder in a garage – it sounded really dodgy to me. And Oscar looks so young. What if he's come from a puppy farm?"

Amy gasped. "Seriously? You think he could have?"

"Well, it's a possibility. And if I'm right, there could be others coming down with this awful sickness. And if they don't get the right help, and quickly…" Leah trailed off.

Amy stared at her in horror. "Carrie's mum said the ad was in the local paper." "We could go back to the B&B, see if we've still got it."

Suddenly, Leah was dashing off, round to the side of the house.

"What are you doing?" Amy cried. She followed her friend and found her by the recycling bins, rooting through a stack of papers.

"Here it is!" Leah cried, pulling a newspaper from the stack and riffling through it to the ads at the back. "This is it. Carrie's dad's circled the ad, look!"

Amy peered over Leah's shoulder. The advert just said "Labrador puppies for sale – ready now," and gave the breeder's number, a mobile.

"Come on, we have to get down to the vet's and talk to Kate," said Leah. "She'll know what to do. I'll give you a backie."

Amy looked reluctantly at Leah's rickety old mountain bike, but she knew there was no time to lose, so she climbed on to the seat. Leah stood up on the pedals and after a shaky start, they set off down the road.

When they got to the vet's, Kate told them that Carrie and her mum were still talking to Mr Ellis in his consulting room, but that Oscar would definitely be staying in to be cared for. "He's in a terrible state, the poor little thing," she said sadly.

"Do you know what this awful illness is?" asked Amy anxiously.

"I'm afraid it's been confirmed as parvovirus," said Kate.

"What's that?" Amy asked.

Kate frowned. "It's a terrible disease," she said. "It causes all the symptoms that you saw – high fever, vomiting and diarrhoea."

Leah gasped. "Can you cure it?"

Kate grimaced. "There's no cure as such," she told them. "And I'm afraid to say, it can be deadly," she added, in a whisper.

Amy felt sick. "But Oscar... We got him to you in time, didn't we? Surely he'll be OK now he's getting treatment?"

"Mr Ellis and his team will do the absolute best they can. But with Oscar being only six weeks old..."

"I knew it!" cried Leah crossly. "I thought he looked too young to be away from his mother! You know, Carrie's dad bought him from a man at a garage!"

"Leah thinks he could have come from a puppy farm," Amy told Kate, in a low voice.

"I hate to say this, but I think you might

be right," said Kate. "Parvovirus is associated
with them, because of the unhygienic
conditions the puppies are kept in. And two
other male puppies were brought in earlier
in the week by owners in the area, both six
weeks old, and both with the same illness."

Leah went pale.

"They could be Oscar's brothers," Amy
gasped. "Oh, the poor little things. How are
they now? Please don't say…"

"No, no, they survived, thank goodness,"
said Kate quickly. "They're at home with their
owners, recovering. But it was touch and go."

"I hope Oscar will be as lucky," Amy
murmured.

"In the light of what you girls have said,
I'll contact the other two owners and ask
how they got their puppies, and try to get
the contact number for the breeder from
them, so I can pass it all on to the RSPCA,"
Kate said. "I'm snowed under, but I have a

bit of time later – just before we close…"

"*We* could do something right now," Leah offered eagerly.

"No way. I'll deal with it," said Kate firmly.

"OK," said Leah.

Amy thought that she'd backed down very quickly. Suspiciously quickly, in fact.

Kate must have thought so, too, because she said, "I'm serious, Leah. I know what you're like. This could be dangerous territory – you have to leave it up to the RSPCA."

"We will," Leah promised. "Puppy farming is a very nasty business."

"OK, good. Right, well, I have to get on – like I said, I'm snowed under today." With that, she hurried off with an armful of files.

When she was safely out of earshot, Amy turned to her friend. "If you were serious about not getting involved," she said, "then why didn't you just give Kate the breeder's phone number?"

Leah patted her back pocket, which held the torn-out advert. "I will, later," she said. "But, Amy, Kate said herself she can't work on this yet, and it would really help if we could get some concrete evidence for the RSPCA in the meantime..."

"Oh no," said Amy. "Leah, what are you planning?"

"I don't know yet," said her friend. "But we can't stand around here doing nothing. Come on."

"But shouldn't we wait for Carrie and her mum?" asked Amy. "See if there's any more news about Oscar?"

Leah frowned. "We can't do anything for Oscar at the moment," she told her. "But there could be other puppies suffering right now. And we might be able to help them."

That was enough to convince Amy. "All right," she said, "let's head back to yours and come up with a plan."

CHAPTER THREE

Amy and Leah arrived back at the stables, grabbed themselves some juice from the fridge, then went up to Leah's room.

"Leah, I'm having second thoughts about this," Amy said, as she sat down on the fluffy rug. "Let's leave it to Kate rather than trying to come up with a plan."

But Leah just grinned. "Well, I already *have* come up with a plan," she told her.

Amy groaned, but Leah's eyes were gleaming. "We call the breeder and pretend we want to buy a pup, and arrange to meet him at the garage on the main road, just like Carrie's dad did. Then I'll go and talk to him while you hide and get pictures of him with the puppy. Oh, and make sure you get one of the car licence plate as well…"

"But that sounds dangerous!" Amy cried.

"Shh!" went Leah. "Someone might hear. If any of my family get wind of what we're doing, they'll put a stop to it."

"What we're doing? I haven't agreed to anything yet!" Amy hissed. "What if the breeder gets suspicious? If he can treat animals in such a terrible way, who knows what he might do to us!"

"We'll be in a public place," Leah reasoned. "If there are any problems, we'll just run into the garage."

"Well, maybe," Amy said tentatively. "We'd have to get there before him, so I can make sure I'm hidden."

"Ah! So you're saying you'll do it, then?"

Leah asked eagerly.

"Do what?" said George. Amy and Leah looked round to find him standing in the doorway, then they glanced at each other.

"Oh, nothing," Leah stammered. "Just, I wanted us to try this ... erm ... line-dancing class and Amy isn't sure..."

"Oh, right," said George. "I just came to get my MP3 player back." He took it from Leah's window sill, and the girls gave him big false smiles until he'd gone, shutting the door behind him.

"Phew, that was close!" gasped Leah.

"Line dancing?" giggled Amy.

Leah shrugged. "I don't know – it just popped into my head. So, anyway, can I use your phone? I'll call the breeder now."

Amy pulled her mobile out of her trouser pocket and handed it to Leah. "But what if he thinks you sound too young and doesn't take you seriously?" she asked. "Maybe if

41

we told George, he'd…"

Leah shook her head. "We can't risk him telling Mum and Dad," she said firmly. "We have to keep this to ourselves and hope the breeder takes the bait."

Leah pulled the crumpled piece of newspaper from her pocket, smoothed it out and dialled the number. Amy went to stand by the door, to listen for anyone else coming upstairs.

"Oh, yes, hello, I saw your ad about puppies for sale," said Leah. Pause. "Yes. Daddy's agreed that I can have one for my birthday tomorrow, so we were really hoping to get it today…"

Leah rolled her eyes, and Amy knew she was finding it really hard to act so naïve. "Daddy? Yes, he's here, hold on." She paused and made a play of walking round looking for him. "Oh, actually, he's just on the other line at the moment, but if you can wait a few minutes…"

The girls both held their breath. If the breeder insisted on speaking to Leah's dad then they were sunk.

"No, that's fine," Leah said at last, giving Amy the thumbs up. "Yes, in cash, that's fine. Where do you live? We'll come straight over. Oh, in Portho? That's a long way…"

Just as had happened with Carrie's mum, when Leah told the breeder that she lived

in White Horse Bay, he offered to meet her
(and, as he thought, her dad) in the garage
on the main road just outside the village.
"He said he'd be an hour," Leah told Amy,
once she'd hung up. "He'll be driving a blue
pick-up truck." She looked excited, but
Amy's stomach flipped over and she felt
like she was going to be sick.

Half an hour later, they set off for the
meeting. Rufus, who'd made up his mind to
come along for the ride, bounded happily
beside them. They'd tried to get him to go
back to the yard, but he absolutely wouldn't
leave them, so they'd decided that he could
hide with Amy while Leah spoke to the
breeder. Amy borrowed George's bike (they
told him it was to go to a line-dancing class
in the village community centre!) and just
as they were about to leave the yard, he
came rushing out of the house, waving his
rucksack. He handed it to Leah. "You

haven't got hats, you need cowboy hats for line dancing," he told her. "Here, take the ones me and Dad got from that Western riding day."

Leah peered into the rucksack and was about to protest, but Amy just took it, said thanks very much and pulled it on to her shoulders.

They got to the garage fifteen minutes before the agreed meeting time so that Amy could find a good place to hide. Luckily it was just a small local garage and there were only a few parking spaces to one side. Amy found a bench on the grass verge behind them, half hidden by an overgrown hedge. It was a space for people to stop off to stretch their legs and let their dogs out of the car for a while, so she looked right at home there with Rufus in tow.

A battered blue pick-up truck pulled into a parking space a few minutes early, taking the girls by surprise. "Are you ready?" Amy hissed, ducking down so that the driver wouldn't see that they were together.

"Yes, I'm ready!" cried Leah. "Ready to give him a piece of my mind! Forget our plan, I'm just going to go and tell him exactly what an awful state Oscar's in, and those other puppies, all thanks to his greed—"

"Leah!" Amy hissed. "Look, if you can't keep a cool head I think *I'd* better go. You stay here with Rufus."

Leah sighed and nodded. "You're right," she said. "There's no way I could be that close to him and not say something."

Amy handed Leah Rufus's lead and a camera. "I'll glance over after a few minutes," she told her. "Give me a signal if you've got all the photos we need. When you have, go to the payphone and ring me."

"Will do," said Leah. "Good luck."

"Thanks," said Amy. She steeled herself and strode over to the pick-up.

A man with sandy-coloured hair and dusty jeans got out. "Where's your dad?" he asked, looking around suspiciously.

"Oh, he had some work stuff to sort out; something urgent came up, that's why he was on the phone when you rang," Amy lied, thinking on her feet. "I wanted to ride my bike down, so he's meeting me here. He won't be a minute. Can I see the puppy?"

Her heart was pounding and her mouth was dry. She was sure the man was going to get back in the truck and drive off. But, instead, he opened the passenger side door and got a puppy out of a box. It looked the same size as Oscar, which Amy knew from Kate meant it was only about six weeks old, far too young to be away from its mother.

Amy bit back her awkward questions,

and forced herself to say, "Aw, he's so cute!"
as she stroked the puppy's velvety head.

"She," said the man. "Female."

"Perfect!" Amy crooned, trying to sound
really ditzy. "I've always wanted a girl dog.
I was so happy when Daddy agreed to buy
me one." She held the puppy up in front of
her, so that Leah could get some good
pictures. "Oh, you are cute, aren't you?" she
cooed. "Yes, you are! You are!"

"Look, where's your dad?" the man demanded, glancing twitchily around him. "I can't wait all day."

"He should be here any second," said Amy. She sensed that time was running out. She stole a quick glance at Leah, who gave her a nod. Then she saw her hurry towards the payphone.

A couple of minutes passed, during which Amy gabbled on about her birthday and the puppy, so that the breeder couldn't get a word in edgeways. Then finally, her phone rang. "Oh," she said, "let me just…" She cradled the puppy in one arm so she could pull the phone from her pocket with her free hand. "Where are you?" she cried, pretending to speak to her dad. "But you're supposed to be… What, all day? But you promised…"

Amy didn't need to say more. The breeder snatched the puppy from her and strode back

round to the driver's side of the pick-up
truck. "Blimmin' time-wasters!" he grumbled
as he put the puppy back in the box and got
in. He started the engine and reversed so
quickly Amy had to jump out of the way.

Leah and Rufus came rushing over. "Are
you OK?" Leah gasped. "He nearly hit you!"

"I'm fine," said Amy shakily. She could
still almost feel the gorgeous little pup
wiggling in her arms. "It broke my heart,
having to let him take that puppy back…"
she mumbled.

"Don't worry, it'll be OK," said Leah
firmly. "I've got pictures of that ratbag, the
licence plate, everything… Look." She
handed the camera back to Amy, who
scrolled through the photos, impressed.
Then Amy looked up as Leah said, "Hang
on a minute…" She was peering up the
road, after the truck. "He just turned down
that track, I'm sure of it!"

"But that doesn't make sense," said Amy. "He's supposed to be going back to Portho."

"It could have been a lie!" gasped Leah. "An excuse to stop people seeing the puppies with their mother. I'm even more convinced something dodgy's going on now. And it means we can follow him – the track behind us leads on to the lane he turned down. We can catch him up. Come on!"

Before Amy could stop her, Leah had leaped on to her bike and she and Rufus were racing off down the gravel track.

"Leah, we're way out of our depth here!" Amy cried, springing on to George's bike and following her friend. Despite her fears, she wouldn't let Leah go alone.

CHAPTER FOUR

The girls shot on to the lane and spotted the pick-up truck just a little way ahead of them. They were both pedalling as hard as they could, and luckily the lane was very windy, so the pick-up couldn't go too fast. Still, as they hit an uphill stretch, it pulled away from them. "Come on!" cried Leah. "We can't let him get away now!"

"I'm going as fast as I can!" gasped Amy. Even Rufus was panting hard, and looked like he was going to collapse at any moment.

"Face it, Leah, we're going to lose him,"

wheezed Amy, as the pick-up reached the
brow of the hill. But, just then, a hay lorry
pulled right out in front of it, making the
breeder beep the horn angrily – and
slowing him right down.

Leah turned and grinned at Amy. "Luck
is on our side!" she called.

Amy couldn't help grinning, too, as they
caught the breeder up. They had to make
sure they stayed a little way back, so he
didn't notice them following. A few minutes
later, he turned off the lane on to a bumpy
driveway overhung with thick bushes. The
girls and Rufus stopped for a rest as they
watched the truck disappear down it. In the
distance they could see a scruffy old house
on some land all by itself.

"That's the only house down there," said
Amy. "So now we know where he lives, and
where he's keeping the puppies." She
pulled her phone from her pocket. "Right,

let's call the RSPCA. We can direct them straight here."

"We could," said Leah. "But now we're here I think we should just sneak down the drive, wait until he goes inside and then have a look around, in case there are any more puppies."

Amy gave her a look of absolute horror. "But we could be putting ourselves in serious danger," she cried. "No one even knows where we are!"

"We'll be fine," Leah insisted. "Look, this is our chance to get real concrete evidence. If our suspicions are right and it's a puppy farm, we could take pictures, and get the place shut down now, today."

Amy sighed. Her fears were still there, but the thought of poor Oscar gave her courage. "Let's be quick, then," she said.

The girls freewheeled down the bumpy drive, with Rufus trotting along beside them.

They spotted the blue pick-up truck
parked by the front door, but they couldn't
see the man anywhere outside. "Let's find a
way round the back," whispered Leah.

The girls walked their bikes down a side
path and propped them against a tree.
Then Leah tied Rufus's lead round its trunk
and told him to keep quiet. Amy thought
he'd bark and want to go with them, but he
was so tired out that he gratefully flopped
to the ground without any protest.

Amy and Leah shared a glance. "Ready?"
asked Leah.

"As I'll ever be," Amy replied. "Let's go."

Crouching down, they snuck up to the
house and looked into one of the windows,
but they just saw an ordinary living room.
They hurried to the next window and peered
in. The curtains were drawn, but there was a
small gap between them. They both gasped
in shock at what they saw, and Amy clapped

her hand over her mouth to stop herself
from crying out in horror. They were looking
into a tiny, dirty room, where there were two
puppies with their mother and another two
adult dogs, all of them crammed in together.
The water bowl in the corner was empty and
they didn't even have a blanket between
them, never mind beds. The two adult dogs
without puppies were lying on their sides,
staring into space. One of the dogs was in a
puddle of her own wee, and there was poo
in the corner. Amy's stomach lurched – she'd
never seen anything so awful in her life.

"How can anyone treat animals like this?" whispered Leah, her voice choking up in her throat. The window was on a latch, opened a crack for air. Leah pulled at it, but it wouldn't move.

The two puppies weren't playing as they should have been, either. Instead, they were lying down too, huddled up against their mother. Suddenly, one of them vomited. Its mother turned her head, but she was too weak to clean the puppy up.

Leah shuddered.

Amy's heart lurched. She felt like smashing the window and climbing in to help. "They've got the sickness, too," she whispered, tears running down her cheeks now. For a moment, she felt completely desperate, lost for what to do, but then she pulled herself together. "Let's take some photos and get out of here," she hissed. "We can call the RSPCA from the lane.

They'll come straight away now we've seen with our own eyes what's going on."

"But we can't just leave the dogs," Leah croaked, looking as desperate as Amy felt.

"I don't want to, either, but it's not for long," Amy told her, while taking pictures with the camera. "Think about it, Leah. These people are dangerous. If they can treat animals like this, what will they do if they find us snooping around?"

"I know, but—" Suddenly, Leah grabbed Amy's arm and pulled her down below the level of the window sill. The breeder had thrown the door open and was striding into the room, with the puppy he'd shown Amy in one of his huge hands. If Leah had been a second slower, he'd have seen them.

"Bring a cloth!" he bellowed, making both girls jump. "One of the dogs has been sick."

A woman shuffled in behind him and

hurriedly began to clean up the mess. "These two don't look too good," she mumbled, frowning at the puppies.

"I can see that!" the breeder snapped at her. "I was hoping to sell them this week, but I won't be able to, not in this state!"

Amy and Leah stared at each other in disbelief. He didn't sound concerned at all, just annoyed.

"Maybe we should take them to a vet," the woman suggested timidly.

"Don't be stupid," the breeder said gruffly. "There would be too many questions, and besides, think of the cost. We'll just have to hope they get better, at least enough so they can be sold."

Leah gasped in horror at that and then clapped her hand over her mouth.

"What was that noise?" growled the breeder.

"Just the pipes, probably," said the woman.

The man stood there listening, and the girls stayed still, hardly daring to breathe. Then, after what felt like a lifetime, he said, "Yeah, probably nothing." Seconds later they heard the pair leave the room, shutting the door behind them.

Tentatively, Leah bobbed up and stole a glance in the window. "They've gone," she whispered, her voice shaking.

Amy saw that they'd put the healthy puppy back in. She was whimpering and looking in bewilderment at the other poor little puppies.

"Leah, they're just going to leave them to … to…"

Amy didn't have to say anything more. The girls looked at each other, then grabbed the window frame and began wrenching at it with all their strength. The catch broke and Amy gave Leah a leg up, as if she was helping her mount Nutmeg. Leah heaved herself across the open window, then swung her legs inside. The adult dogs didn't bark, thank goodness, but just cowered a little. One of them gazed out at Amy with such a sad, desperate look that she thought her heart would break.

"Don't worry, we're here to help," Leah whispered. She picked up one of the ill puppies and handed him out of the window to Amy. "We'll get your two poorly puppies to the vet's, then we'll be back for the other puppy and the rest of you, too. Promise."

Leah passed the second ill puppy to Amy and then climbed back out of the window.

The girls hurriedly placed the puppies into George's backpack, laying them on the upturned cowboy hats. Then Leah tightened the toggle just enough so that they could look out, but not fall.

They hurried back to the tree, untied Rufus, and leaped on to their bikes. They pedalled along by the side of the house and were just about to ride on to the drive when they heard voices. They both put the brakes on and stayed still, listening. It was the breeder and the woman, and they seemed to be having some kind of argument. Amy followed the sound and her stomach lurched as she spotted them on the driveway. "Leah, they're right in our way! We'll never get the puppies out now!" she hissed.

"See, there's no one here, you're just being paranoid!" shouted the woman.

"I'm sure I heard something," countered the man. "I think we've got a trespasser.

We need to do a search. I'll go round the far side and you look down there."

The girls gasped in horror as he gestured towards the side path, just where they were standing.

How on earth were they going to get away now?

Suddenly, Amy had an idea. "You'll have to distract them," she whispered. "Keep them talking round the front and I'll sneak off up the driveway with these two. Pretend you were out for a bike ride with Rufus and got lost. Ask for directions, talk about the weather, anything. Just keep them looking the other way until I'm out of sight."

At first Leah looked terrified about the idea of going right up to the nasty couple, but then she steeled herself and nodded. She got off her bike and wheeled it across to them, with Rufus beside her. "Hello? Oh, thank goodness I've found someone!"

she cried. "I was out on a bike ride with my dog and I got lost."

"Where have you come from?" Amy heard the man demand, making her feel sick with worry for Leah.

"Oh, down there, over the field," said Leah casually, gesturing to the furthest corner of the land, away from the house.

"You're on private property," the man said gruffly.

"Oh sorry," said Leah. "I didn't realize. I…"

Then, "Where are you trying to get to?" asked the woman, a little more gently.

Amy sighed with relief. Leah had convinced them. But for how long, she didn't know. She had to hurry past, right now. Leah had positioned herself so that, in order to look at her, the couple had to face away from the side passage. She was gesturing to the right and left, as was the man, so it looked like their plan to ask for directions was working. Amy felt her heart thudding in her chest as she broke out of the cover of the side path and pedalled as fast as she could for the driveway.

"So, it's through this field, then left and then the next right?" she heard Leah say.

"No, up the drive and then take the track on your right, then left and left again," said the breeder, clearly getting annoyed.

Amy didn't dare look back. She just stood up and pedalled so hard her legs were shaking. As soon as she got back to the lane, she pulled over and called the vet's, while looking anxiously down at the house. She could see Leah, still standing there with Rufus and the terrible pair.

Kate answered after a couple of rings. She started to say "White Horse Bay vet's, how may I—" but Amy cut her off, gabbling about the puppies, and the awful couple, and telling her where they were. Kate didn't ask any questions, she just listened and then she said, "Stay put, I'm on my way right now. I'll be five minutes."

Amy watched anxiously as Leah began to walk away from the couple, heading towards the driveway. "Yes, we've done it!" she gasped, feeling relief flood through her.

The couple were turning to go back into the house. But then… Amy's heart sank.

Something was up, because suddenly the breeder was shouting and swearing, and they were both chasing Leah up the drive. "Leah, look out!" Amy screamed.

Leah glanced behind her and then she and Rufus made a dash for it.

Amy grabbed her bike and got back on, ready to go. The pair were running fast, but Leah was losing them, pedalling as hard as she could. Then Amy saw that the breeder was staring at her, and at the rucksack.

"Hey, she's got our puppies!" he shouted.

Just then, Kate's car came screeching down the lane. Amy dropped her bike and ran to it, wrenched open the passenger door and dived in. Kate pulled into a gateway and turned the car round as Leah ran up and threw herself into the back seat, pulling Rufus in behind her. Just as the nasty couple reached the car, Kate put her foot down and they sped away in a spray of dust and stones.

"I can't believe what just happened! Are you OK?" Amy gasped. Leah nodded, panting hard.

"Call the vet's," said Kate, as they headed back into the village. "Get Mr Ellis on standby."

Leah made the call. "He'll be ready for us," she told Kate and Amy when she'd spoken to Laura, the veterinary nurse.

A couple of minutes later, they reached the surgery, parked up and rushed inside.

Amy handed the two puppies straight over to Mr Ellis.

"Now that pair know someone's on to them, they might try to move the other dogs. I'll ring the RSPCA right away," Kate told him.

"Good thinking," he said, as he hurried into his consulting room.

The girls were about to follow him, but Kate blocked their path, arms folded. "Not so fast," she said sternly. "What on earth did you think you were playing at, going down there alone? I told you to wait until I could sort things out."

"Sorry, but I'm glad we did it," said Leah, "or it might have been too late for these two."

Amy was suddenly struck with a terrible thought. "It might be too late already..." she said aloud. "It's not, is it? Please, say it's not!"

Kate frowned. "We'll have to see what Mr Ellis says," she told them.

CHAPTER FIVE

The girls were still anxiously waiting an hour later for news of the ill puppies when the phone rang in the vet's surgery. "It's the RSPCA," said Kate, handing it to Mr Ellis. The girls tried to listen in, but they couldn't follow what was being said.

"Did they get to the other dogs in time?" asked Amy, when he put the phone down. She couldn't help thinking back to how one of them had looked right at her with sad, desperate eyes.

"Yes, they did. They've taken them all to

Castlereach Animal Rescue Centre," Mr
Ellis told them. "They've tested for the
virus and the adult dogs have had a
negative result."

Amy and Leah shared a glance of relief.

"Still, they're in a terrible state from
being used as breeding machines. They'll
need lots of care to get back to health," the
vet went on. "One of them is expecting a
litter of puppies in a couple of weeks, too."

"Oh, goodness!" cried Leah. "It's so lucky
she was rescued. To think, it would have
just carried on and on…"

"What about the other puppy? The one I
held at the garage?" asked Amy, thinking
back to how the puppy had felt in her arms.

"She's showing no signs of infection so
far," Mr Ellis told her. "So fingers crossed
she hasn't picked up the virus. She'll go to
one of their volunteers' homes to be kept in
quarantine for two weeks. If she doesn't

show symptoms in that time, she should be fine."

"And what happened to those awful people?" asked Kate.

"Pete, the RSPCA officer I just spoke to, caught them trying to leave," he told her. "They're being questioned by the police now."

"Good," Leah snapped. "I hope they lock them up and throw away the key. I don't know how anyone can treat animals like that!"

"I agree with you, Leah," said Mr Ellis, "but that doesn't mean you can take matters into your own hands. When I think what could have happened! Oh, and Pete said they brought your bikes back with them, too. He'll bring them over when he comes to do the paperwork for the puppies you rescued. Right, I've got to go and scrub up before my home visits. Laura's taken the puppies through to the isolation ward. Can you get the forms ready for Pete, Kate?"

Kate looked up from behind the desk.
"Yes, of course," she said. "And Hannah's
already started disinfecting the consulting
room, then she'll do in here." She turned to
the girls. "We have to be really careful we
get rid of every trace of this virus," she
explained, "otherwise another dog could
pick it up when it comes in."

With that, Mr Ellis strode off.

"Pete won't be long," Kate told them,
"then you can get your bikes back and head
home."

"Actually," said Leah. "I was thinking of
ringing Mum to ask if she can take us over
to the rescue centre in Castlereach to see
the mother dogs. It'll mean coming clean
about what we've done, but it'll be worth it
to be able to help out with them."

"I would leave it for the moment," said
Kate. "It's great that you want to help, but

the staff there will be busy doing medical and behavioural assessments, cleaning the dogs up and sorting them out. I'm off tomorrow, and I'd love to help, too. I'll give them a ring if you like, see if we can all go over in the morning. How does that sound?"

Amy looked at Leah. She knew her friend wanted to get straight over there, but she also knew that Kate was right – if they went now, they'd probably only be in the way.

"Well, in that case I'm going to stay here and wait for news about the two ill puppies," Leah announced, sitting back down on a plastic chair.

"No, you aren't," said Kate firmly. "They'll be here for days, and there really is nothing you can do. Look, I'll let you know as soon as there's any news. Pete will be here in a minute and I haven't even started this form." She pulled a pen from the pot on the reception desk. "Right, we need names for the two puppies. Would you like to do the honours?"

Amy thought for a moment. "Erm, how about Lucky for the girl?" she suggested, "because she'll need all her luck to survive this."

"Oh, and I like Scout for the boy," said Leah. "It makes me think of him jumping about in fields, which has to be a good sign."

"OK, Lucky and Scout it is," said Kate, writing the names down.

Soon Pete arrived and the girls got their bikes back (and another telling-off for facing the breeders alone). Then they set off for White Horse Stables, after making Kate promise once again to let them know the second there was any news on Lucky and Scout, and Oscar, of course.

When the girls arrived back at the stables, Amy was about to call her mum to come and collect her when Leah said, "Why don't you ask if you can stay here tonight? Neither of us are going to sleep anyway, what with worrying about the puppies. And that way, if Kate rings with any news, we'll be together to hear it."

"Good idea," said Amy. "I'll have to tell Mum everything that's been going on, though," she added. "I know I'll get into trouble, but if we want to go to the rescue centre tomorrow, I'll have to explain why."

"Me too," said Leah. "I guess we'd better get it over with."

So Leah walked off over to the yard to find Rosie and Dan, and Amy called her mum. Both girls explained the situation (toning down the bit where they put themselves in danger!). They did each get a telling-off, but luckily both Amy's mum and Rosie agreed that Amy could stay over.

As Rosie loaded the dishwasher after tea, Amy and Leah sat at the kitchen table, staring at Amy's phone.

"Look, why don't I take you out for a hack?" Rosie suggested. "It's a lovely evening, and I don't have any lessons to teach. We could ask Billy, too – he's still around on the yard."

"But we're waiting to hear from Kate," Leah began.

"Bring your phone, Amy," Rosie suggested. "If there's any news, you'll know

straight away. Come on, it would do you
both good, after the day you've had. Take
your minds off it." At that, Amy prepared
herself for another telling-off, but Rosie
didn't say anything more, luckily.

"Well, it would be nice to spend some
time with Nutmeg," said Leah.

So, an hour later, the girls had tacked up
Gracie and Nutmeg and were riding down
to the beach with Rosie on her horse, Cody,
and Billy on Spark. Trotting along beside
the waves was great fun and Amy managed
to forget her worries for a while. She knew
Leah was feeling better, too, because she
gave her a huge grin and cried, "Let's
canter!" Before Amy could answer, Leah
and Nutmeg were zooming off down the
beach.

"Want a go?" Rosie asked Amy.

Amy grinned at her. "Yes, please!"

Rosie looked at Billy and he nodded. "Let's go, then!" she cried, moving into canter. Amy sat down and put her legs back, then she and Gracie were off, too. It was amazing, cantering along by the waves, with Rosie and Billy riding beside her, a little way up the sand. As they caught up with Leah, she turned and cried, "Way to go!" then she slowed a little so that Amy could ride next to her. The girls were grinning at one another, but perhaps they should have been looking ahead, because

when Amy faced forward again she saw a
big piece of driftwood looming in front of
her. She thought about going round it, but
Leah was alongside her, and there wasn't
time for both of them to move.

"Leah, what do I—" she began, feeling
panicky.

"We'll have to… JUMP!" cried Leah, and
both Nutmeg and Gracie reached the
driftwood at once and leaped over. For a
moment, Amy felt like they were flying – it
was a fabulous feeling. Then they hit the
ground and she had a little wobble, but she

managed to stay on and bring Gracie back to a trot, and then through walk to halt.

Rosie and Billy slowed down, too. "Go Amy!" whooped Billy.

"Well done!" cried Rosie.

Amy gave Gracie a big pat. "I can't believe I just did that," she gasped.

Leah giggled. "You weren't expecting to get another go at jumping so soon, were you!" she cried.

Soon after they got back to the yard, Amy's mum arrived to drop her things off. She stayed to have a cup of tea with Rosie and Dan before giving Amy a big hug and then heading back to the B&B.

Later on, Amy and Leah watched a DVD while keeping a close eye on Amy's phone. They even managed to enjoy the film a bit. But when Amy was lying on Leah's fluffy rug in her sleeping bag, all her worries about the puppies came crowding back in. "Oh, there's no way I'll be able to sleep," she sighed.

"Me neither," Leah groaned, turning over in her bed for the tenth time.

Too tired to talk much, they both lay there for what felt like hours. When Amy's phone rang she was sure she hadn't slept at all, but when she saw that it was 5am, she realized she must have drifted off at some point.

"Amy? It's Kate."

"Oh, er, hi," she mumbled, rubbing her face and leaning over to shake Leah awake. She felt suddenly sick, expecting the worst.

"The three puppies were doing OK when I left at seven last night and no one's called me to say that's changed," Kate assured her. Amy gave an anxious-looking Leah the thumbs up and held the phone between

83

them so that her friend could hear, too. "We can call and get an update at eight o'clock when the surgery opens," Kate said. "I'm calling now because the pregnant dog's having her puppies…"

"What?" gasped Amy. "But I thought they weren't due for another couple of weeks…"

"That's what everyone thought," said Kate. "When I spoke to the rescue centre after you left yesterday, I offered to help anytime with any of the dogs and they've called for me to go in. It's all hands on deck."

"Wow, that's amazing," said Amy, feeling a little envious.

But then Kate said, "And I asked them if you could help too, and they said yes, so I'm picking you up in fifteen minutes."

Amy's stomach flipped over with excitement. Helping out with newborn puppies? She couldn't believe it!

"Great!" cried Leah, fully awake by now. "See you soon!"

Leah went to tell Rosie what was happening and when she said they could go, the girls hurriedly got dressed and went down to the hall to wait for Kate.

CHAPTER SIX

"Aw, he's gorgeous!" Leah cooed, as Alex, the rescue centre worker, rubbed down the last little puppy to be born with a towel and tucked him in next to his mother.

"But they're so tiny!" gasped Amy.

"They will need a lot of extra care," said Sian, the rescue centre owner, who had helped deliver the puppies with Alex.

The girls and Kate had arrived just in time to see the last two being born, and there were six in all.

"Because the mother – Mabel, we've

decided to call her – was in such poor health, she's got a low milk supply," Sian explained. "We'll have to hand-feed the puppies as well, to make sure they're getting enough nutrition. Alex, do you mind bringing some milk kits down from the storeroom?" she asked. "With the girls here to help we could start now."

Soon, Amy and Leah were sitting side by side with a newborn puppy each in their arms, feeding them with special puppy milk, while Kate went with Sian to prepare a nice, cosy indoor pen for them all. After that they had to clean around each puppy's bottom to encourage them to wee and poo – Sian explained that the mother dog would usually do this, but poor Mabel was so weak that she was struggling to manage with six pups. They also had to spend time with each one, picking them up and cuddling them to keep them warm and stimulated.

"I think you've got the best job in the world," Leah told Alex as she cuddled one of the puppies close.

"It's bittersweet," said Alex. "There are lots of happy endings when we find new homes for our rescues, but sometimes we see terrible things along the way, and some dogs never recover enough from the traumas in their lives to be rehomed."

Amy gasped. "That's awful." She couldn't help thinking about Lucky and Scout, fighting for their lives at the vet's. And the other pup still in quarantine. Would they even make it far enough to be rehomed? And would Oscar get back to Carrie? "How are the other two adult dogs the RSPCA brought in?" she asked Alex.

"Millie and Maeve?" he asked. "That's what we've called them. They've been bathed and checked over, and treated for fleas and worms, and they're getting back on their feet again, but they're still very weak and frightened. I'll take you to see them later, if you like."

"Yes, please," said Amy. She just wanted to give them a big cuddle and tell them that everything would be OK now.

Leah looked from the gorgeous little newborn puppy in her arms to poor Mabel, their mother. Amy knew she was thinking of Oscar, Lucky and Scout as well. "I just don't understand how anyone could put animals through such pain and suffering just to make a profit," she muttered. "It makes me so angry."

"That's why I do this job," said Alex. "I feel like at least I'm trying to do something about the terrible cruelty that goes on."

Kate was watching the clock as much as Amy and Leah, and at eight on the dot she called the vet's to get an update on the three puppies. "They're all hanging in there, but they're not well enough to leave the vet's yet," she told them, as soon as she'd spoken to Laura, the veterinary nurse.

"Well, at least it's not bad news," Amy told Leah. She knew they'd both been hoping for something better, though.

The rescue centre staff had started to arrive by then and two of them, Jack and Chloe, came to take over so that the girls could have a break. Alex took them down to the staff room and got them both glasses of juice and some toast and cereal. "We're quite often here at night for one reason or another," he told them. "So Sian keeps us stocked up with breakfast things."

When they'd finished, he took them to see Millie and Maeve. Both dogs looked much better already, with their coats clean and their nails clipped, lying on comfy beds rather than the bare floor. When the girls went into their pen, Millie wagged her tail and came over to them. Maeve, the dog who'd given Amy such a sad look when they'd seen her in that awful room, didn't get up. In fact, she hardly even moved when Amy went over and gently stroked her.

"Maeve's struggling to form a bond with people," Alex told them. "She's been like this with all of us. We hope she'll come round in time, but if she doesn't respond to anyone, it's going to make it very difficult to rehome her."

Amy felt sick. "Do you think she might be one of those cases you were talking about?" she asked. "The ones that never recover enough from the traumas in their lives?"

"I hope not," said Alex, "but that's my worry, yes."

Amy had a sudden thought and at first she felt too shy to ask, but then she glanced at poor Maeve again and it gave her all the courage she needed. "Maybe I could spend some time with her?" she suggested. "I could try and get her to come out of her shell."

"That would be great," Alex said. "We spend as much time as we can with the dogs, of course, but we're always so busy round here. It would be lovely for her to have someone to work with one-on-one. I can give you any help you need."

Amy smiled, feeling excitement bubble up inside her. "Thanks."

"Shall we get back to the puppies now?" Leah asked, giving Millie's head a final stroke.

"I think I'll stay here with Maeve, if that's OK," said Amy.

"No worries," said Leah.

"Why don't we bring her round to the office, so you're not all on your own down here," Alex suggested. "There's plenty of space to work with her there."

So Leah headed back to the puppies, and Alex walked Maeve very slowly up the path and led her round behind the reception desk into the office area. Amy found a comfy corner and sat on the sofa. She took

Maeve's lead from Alex, who gave her a smile, then hurried off.

"You're so lovely," she told Maeve, as she stroked her. "I know you'll have such a wonderful time with your very own new family to love you." She chatted away for ages, but Maeve didn't even look up. Amy tried to interest her in some treats that Chloe brought over, but she didn't even sniff them. Instead, she just lay on the floor, staring into space.

"Oh, look, Maeve, what's this?" said Amy, spotting a squeaky bone-shaped toy on one of the desks and bringing it over. She held it up to Maeve's face. "Look, this is fun, do you want to chew it?" she asked brightly. She squeaked the toy, but Maeve didn't even blink. Amy sighed. "Maybe you'd like to go for a little walk," she suggested. "Come on, then."

Maeve wouldn't get to her feet, though.

Amy knelt down and stroked her. Her coat was much less matted now, but there were big bare patches where she'd been allergic to all the fleas she'd had. And she was terribly thin. Amy knew the hair would grow back in time, and that Maeve would put on weight, and that her eyes and coat would get shinier, thanks to good food.

Yes, she'd get better, on the outside. But would she ever get better on the inside? Would she ever be able to form a bond with someone? Amy remembered Maeve looking right into her eyes from that awful room, just in that moment of surprise as Leah came through the window. She'd made a connection with her then, she was sure of it, but now there was nothing. Would Maeve have the bright future she so deserved?

"How's it going?" asked Alex, popping back in and pulling Amy away from her thoughts.

She grimaced. "Not great. I've tried stroking her, talking to her, giving her toys and treats and even trying to take her for a walk, but she's not responding to anything."

"It's early days yet," Alex said. "Don't worry about achieving anything at this point, it's just good that you're spending time with her – showing her that not all humans are cruel."

He gave Amy a smile, grabbed a file from one of the desks and headed out. As she stroked Maeve, she thought about what he'd said. "That's what I need to do," she told her. "Not try so hard, but just be with you." And suddenly she had an idea and knew exactly how to do that. It would have to be tomorrow, though. She'd need to collect some things from home first.

A few minutes later, Leah bounded in. "I love being on puppy duty!" she declared. "Are you nearly ready to go? Mum's picking me up and she's arranged to drop you home, too."

Amy ruffled Maeve's coat. "Actually, I'd like to stay here all day, but I guess so, yeah." She gave Maeve a final big pat and stroke, even though Maeve acted like she wasn't even there.

Leah gave Maeve a woeful look. "Oh, I wish there was something I could do to stop people going to dodgy breeders out of ignorance or to save money," she said.

"If they realized the suffering of the poor mother dogs they probably wouldn't go," Amy replied, stroking Maeve's ears.

"If only people knew what danger signs to look out for—" Leah was saying, then, "Hi, any news?" she asked, as Kate popped her head round the doorway.

"I've called the vet's again," Kate told them. "They've heard that the female puppy in quarantine is still clear of the disease, and it's good news about Oscar, too. He's over the worst, and he's been able to go home to Carrie and her family, to be looked after there."

"Oh, that's great," said Amy.

"What about Lucky and Scout?" Leah asked.

Kate frowned. "Not so good, I'm afraid. Lucky's pulling round, but Scout's just not responding to the treatment."

Amy gasped. "Oh, that's awful!" she cried. "The poor little thing."

"I just wish there was some way we could help him," said Leah.

"There isn't anything you can do at the vet's," said Kate. "But you're helping a lot, by being here with the other dogs."

"I can't wait to come back tomorrow," said Amy. "I want to do as much as possible to help, same as you, Leah. And I'm determined to make a difference for Maeve."

CHAPTER SEVEN

"We're just going to hang out today, no pressure to do doggie things," Amy told Maeve the next morning. "I'm going to sit here and sketch you."

Once again, they were in the office area behind the reception desk.

Maeve didn't respond, but Amy got her pencil tin and drawing pad out anyway. She spent a long time making a really detailed sketch, and as she did, she chatted away. "You know, usually I have the problem of dogs leaping about as I'm trying to draw

them, but not with you," she said, with a
smile. Then she ended up telling Maeve all
about moving to White Horse Bay, and
meeting Leah, and learning to ride, and
how she'd always dreamed of having her
own dog.

A while later, when she glanced up, she
was surprised to find Maeve looking at her
curiously. She wanted to leap up and give
her a big cuddle, but she didn't want to
scare her off. Instead, she just smiled to
herself and carried on drawing.

Another twenty minutes and the picture of Maeve was finished. "There," said Amy, holding it up for her to see. "Aren't you beautiful? I've made your coat really glossy, which it will be soon, and I haven't drawn the bare patches, because they'll be gone in a few weeks." Maeve was looking at her again, and Amy gave her a big smile. "I'm going to go and see if they need a hand with the puppies," she told her. "Give you a break from me rambling on."

To Amy's astonishment, when she headed through to reception, Maeve got up and followed her. "Oh, wow, look!" she said to Alex, who was standing by the reception desk with a couple and their excited-looking daughter.

"That's fantastic!" cried Alex. "And I had a little peek when you were drawing her. I saw her watching you. That's definitely progress, even if it is small steps."

"She's lovely. Is she yours?" asked the little girl.

Amy shook her head. "No, I'm just helping out." She noticed that the girl's father was signing a form, and her mum was writing out a cheque.

"And here's Buster," said Alex, as Sian came through from the kennels with a boisterous tan and white cross-breed. He headed straight for the little girl and she made a huge fuss of him, then her mum did, too.

"Buster's going to his new home today," said Alex. "We're delighted that you've chosen him," he told the girl's father. "He's a lovely lad. Call if you have any questions and … have fun!"

The family all thanked him, then headed out of the door with their new dog bouncing around beside them. Amy was really happy for them, of course, but she couldn't help feeling a pang of envy, too. She'd give anything to have her own dog, but Mum had made it more than clear that it wasn't an option.

"Do you think Maeve will improve enough to be rehomed one day?" she asked Alex, who was now busy sorting through a pile of paperwork.

"We can't know at this point," he said, "but you've started to get through to her, so it looks promising. If she can form a bond with you, there's nothing to stop her forming one with a family."

"How's it going?" said Leah, as she strode in, carrying a heap of towels and blankets for the puppies.

"Much better," Amy told her, reaching down to stroke Maeve's head. "I'm going to get her rehomed to a nice family if it takes me all year!"

"She's lucky to have you," Leah told Amy.

"I'm lucky to have her," said Amy, giving Maeve another pat. Already, she couldn't imagine life without her, but she pushed the thought away. She was determined to get Maeve to a point where she could have a bright future with her very own family, even though it would mean saying goodbye.

Alex must have guessed how Amy was feeling, because he smiled at her and said, "Hey, I bet Leah could use a hand with those puppies."

"Too right!" Leah exclaimed. "We're about to give them their milk. We could use an extra pair of hands!"

Amy smiled despite herself. "Come on, then."

"Wow, they seem to have grown overnight!" Amy exclaimed a few minutes later as Leah handed her one of the wriggling day-old puppies and a little bottle.

"Do you know, these little ones were actually born with a huge load of worms in their tummies, because the poor mothers hadn't been treated for them?" said Leah, as she picked up another wriggling puppy to try to feed him. "I've decided to ring the local paper and complain about those puppy ads you know!"

"Leah, it's not the paper's fault," Amy pointed out. "They can't go and inspect every breeder who places an ad. It's about

people knowing what to look out for. I
mean, if Carrie's dad had asked the right
questions, he'd never have ended up
supporting a puppy farm."

"I suppose you're right," said Leah. She
looked deep in thought for a moment, then
she said, "Talking about the paper's given
me an idea, though. I could ring them and
see if they want to do a story about what
happened. We could show them the
puppies and the mothers and—"

"And talk about how to buy responsibly,
from a proper breeder," Amy cut in eagerly.

"Or better still, not buy a puppy at all and
get a rescue dog instead!" Leah finished.

The girls looked at each other and
grinned. "That sounds like a plan," said Amy.

When Sian came back in with more
puppy milk kits a few moments later, they
told her all about their idea, and she thought
it was brilliant. So Leah popped down to

reception to call the paper. Ten minutes later, she came dancing back in and announced that the journalist she'd spoken to was really keen to come and do an article and photo shoot the following morning.

"That's fantastic!" cried Amy.

"It'll be great publicity for the centre, too," said Sian. "Good thinking, girls!"

"I just want to feel like I'm doing everything I can to put a stop to these terrible puppy farms," said Leah. "Hey, I know, tonight I'll put a list together – what to look out for when buying a puppy, the dos and don'ts. I'll get Kate to help me and I'll persuade them to print that in the paper, too, with the article. Oh, Kate! We were just talking about you!"

Kate had just appeared. "I came to tell you right away—" she began, and the girls looked so terrified that she quickly said, "No, don't worry, it's good news. Scout's improving now, too. Looks like he and Lucky are both going to pull through!"

"That's such a relief," said Sian, as Amy and Leah hugged each other.

They told Kate about the newspaper article and she agreed to help Leah with the dos and don'ts list. Then, in much higher spirits, they all got stuck into feeding the puppies, and giving them lots of fuss and cuddles.

When Amy's mum came to collect the girls about an hour later, they were still full of excitement as they told her their plans for the next day.

"That sounds like a great idea, girls," she told them.

"Could we just go and see Maeve before we go?" Amy asked. "We were busy with the puppies and I didn't realize the time. I don't want to go without saying goodbye to her. Remember I told you she wasn't responding to me at all? Well, we made loads of progress today – she even followed me when I walked into the reception."

"Oh, that's great," said Mum. She looked at her watch and back at the anxious look on Amy's face. "OK, go on, then, just for a few minutes."

"I'll get a lift back with Kate later," Leah told them. "She's got to stop in and see Mum anyway. Gives me longer with the puppies!" And with that she gave Amy a hug and hurried back up the corridor.

Amy led Mum down to Maeve and Millie's pen. One of the volunteers, Gabby, was standing beside it with two leads in her hand. "Hi, Amy," she said. "I was just about to try and get these two to go for a little walk, to get some strength back, but you can take Maeve if you like. She only needs to go once round the field."

Amy looked hopefully at Mum.

"Go on, then," said Mum, "but after that we'll have to get back. I've got a party of eight arriving this evening and I've only made up two of their rooms so far."

"Thanks, Mum," said Amy, taking the lead from Gabby. When Gabby opened the pen, Millie wandered up to her, tail wagging, and to Amy's amazement, Maeve came up to *her,* too. She made a big fuss of her, and Mum gave her a pat. "Oh, she's lovely, Amy," she said. "The poor thing. What she must have been through."

Amy clipped on the lead, but she didn't really need to. Maeve followed her out of the pen and stayed close as they walked along. "She's doing so well, Alex is hoping she'll be suitable for rehoming one day," Amy said.

"I'm sure she will," said Mum, stooping to ruffle Maeve's coat. "She's such a lovely, gentle girl. I've always liked Labradors."

"Maeve's really bonding with me," Amy said, and then she found herself blurting out, "I know it's difficult, but I was thinking, maybe, *we* could adopt her…"

"Oh, Amy." Mum stopped still and stared at her. "You know we talked about this earlier, love," she whispered, as if she was worried that Maeve might understand. "There's just no way we can take on a dog at the moment – not with all the work at the B&B. Maybe in the future, but now's just not a good time."

"I know … I know you said that," Amy stuttered.

"But Maeve's not just any dog – she's so special and…"

"Amy!" Mum said. "I thought you understood why I've said no to a dog! And with Maeve – well, the insurance would be astronomical because of her health and being a pure breed Lab, and she'd need lots of care and attention. You'll be at school all week and I haven't got time for dog-walking on top of everything else. It wouldn't be fair on her." She glanced down at Maeve, stroked her head and sighed.

Amy stared at the ground, feeling upset. "I know and I'm sorry, she's … she's just really, really special." Amy felt a lump rising in her throat, and she swallowed hard. "I just thought, maybe, you might think about it."

"Well, I'd love to be able to, but you know I can't," said Mum. "Now, come on, let's get Maeve back to her pen."

CHAPTER EIGHT

"Hello, Maeve! How are you this morning!" cried Amy. Rosie had just dropped the girls off at the rescue centre, and Amy had persuaded Leah to come and see Maeve before they did anything else. As they neared her pen, Alex was starting to open it. "Hi, girls!" he called, as Maeve rushed out to greet Amy, head up and tail wagging.

"Morning!" Amy and Leah chorused.

Amy rubbed Maeve's ears and gave her a big pat and stroke. "You're a beautiful girl!" she told her.

"And getting more beautiful every day!" Leah exclaimed. "She looks so much healthier already … and happier!"

"She came up to me this morning, too, and she's had a cuddle with Sian," Alex told them. "She's really responding well to people now, and it's all thanks to you, Amy."

Amy blushed, but she couldn't help smiling.

"I've got some great news," Alex continued. "I've discussed it with Sian and we both want Maeve to feature in your article, with Millie, Mabel and the pups. We think she's ready to be rehomed – isn't that exciting?"

"Yeah, brilliant," cried Leah.

"Great," said Amy, forcing herself to look pleased. And she was, of course. But the idea of not seeing Maeve any more… She made herself push the thought away. It was the best thing for Maeve, she told herself sternly, and that was all that mattered.

Alex headed off to walk Millie round the field, leaving the girls in the courtyard to give Maeve a good brush-down so she looked her best for the photos.

"You're upset, aren't you?" Leah said, trying to catch Amy's eye.

Amy looked at the ground and shrugged, biting back tears.

Leah sighed. "Amy, Maeve will be featured in the paper tomorrow and she's so lovely and sweet, you know she'll be snapped up. If you feel this strongly about her, you'll have to ask to adopt her again. I know your mum's said no loads of times, but if you don't ask you *will* lose her."

"Well…" Amy began.

"Girls," came a voice from behind them. They turned to find Sian standing there. She'd come out of the pen next to Millie and Maeve's. "I don't want to interfere," she said, "but I couldn't help overhearing. We always insist that everyone in the family has to be on board, or the adoption won't work, and it won't be fair on the dog."

"I understand that," Amy mumbled. "I really do. It's just… It's Maeve…"

Sian put her arm round her. "I know it's hard," she said. "But when the time is right, we'll have the perfect dog waiting for you, I'm sure of it."

She is *my perfect dog*, thought Amy. But she just said, "Thanks, Sian." As Sian strode away, Amy finally looked at Leah. "I'll be heartbroken to let Maeve go, but I want her to have a home," she told her. "I wish Mum felt differently, but she doesn't and that's that. So no, I'm not going to ask her again."

Leah smiled sadly. "It's your call," she said.

Amy stood up. "Right, here comes Alex with Millie – you're in charge of making her coat gleam." She grinned cheekily, and added, "Oh, and you could put a brush through your own hair before they get here!"

Leah smirked. "Why bother? It's not me looking for a new home!"

Half an hour later, the journalist Becky Lace arrived with a photographer called Joe. Alex got them cups of coffee and they sat in the staff room and talked to the girls about what had happened when they'd rescued the puppies. Amy felt sick, thinking back to that day, but luckily Leah did most of the talking, and she really managed to get across the true horror of what they'd witnessed. "And we've got photos," Amy added, remembering the pictures she'd taken on her camera just before the nasty breeder had walked into the room.

"Fantastic," said Becky. "We can print before and after pictures in that case, to really get readers into the story, and show them what a great job the centre has done with the rescued dogs."

Amy scrolled through and found one of the pictures. She could hardly look at it as she handed the camera to Becky. Becky and Joe stared at it, and Becky didn't look excited any more, just sickened.

"This is awful," Joe mumbled gruffly. "Disgusting."

ANIMAL S.O.S.

"How are the ill puppies now?" asked Becky anxiously. The girls filled her in on Oscar, Lucky and Scout's recovery, and said that the other girl puppy who was in quarantine at a volunteer's house hadn't come down with the disease so far.

"Fingers crossed she won't," said Amy.

By the time she'd told Becky and Joe about parvovirus, what it did to the poor pups and how life-threatening it was, they looked horrified.

"Let's go and meet the dogs," Leah said cheerily, breaking the shocked silence. "You can see how much they've come on since that awful day."

So Leah showed off the six puppies, and Joe took loads of pictures of them all wriggling over each other, looking adorable, and of Mabel tending to them gently, every inch the proud mum. "What are they called?" asked Becky, notebook at the ready.

"They don't have names yet," said Leah. "I thought maybe we could have a naming competition, as part of the article. Readers could text in their favourite puppy names and we could choose the best."

"That's a great idea," Becky told her. "Then we could do a follow-up report, saying which names were chosen and showing how much the puppies have grown and how they're getting on."

"Brilliant," said Amy. "That will really keep the story in people's minds."

"Oh, and my cousin helped me do this," said Leah, sensing that it was a good time to strike with her list, and handing it over. "It's the dos and don'ts of buying a puppy. You know, how to ask the right questions, and things you should always insist on, like seeing the mother and getting all the right papers. I just thought if people know what they should be looking for, they're less likely to end up unwittingly supporting a puppy farm and all the cruelty that goes with it."

Becky took the list, scanned through it and tucked it into the back of her notepad.

"That's great, Leah," she said. "We'll definitely make space for it."

Amy beamed at her friend. She knew that stopping people buying from puppy farms was what mattered most to her.

After Joe had taken some shots with the girls holding the puppies and stroking Mabel, he said, "Right, I think I've got a good selection here. Shall we go and see the other dogs? There were two more breeding mothers, weren't there?"

"Yes, Millie and Maeve," Leah told him. "Amy's been looking after them, especially Maeve. Come on, I'll lead the way."

When they reached Maeve and Millie's pen, all attention turned to Amy. She felt like running for the hills, but she pushed her shyness away, smiled and started telling Becky and Joe about Millie. She went into the pen and made a fuss of both dogs, then brought Millie out on her lead so that Joe could get some nice pictures of her in the sunshine. Then came the hard part – showing off Maeve.

"So, tell us, Amy, why should someone offer Maeve a new home?" asked Becky, as Joe snapped shots of Amy kneeling next to her, stroking her ears as she wagged her tail and nuzzled her lovingly.

"Erm, well, as you can see, she's got so much love to give," Amy said. "She's calm and gentle, with such a sweet nature. Actually, she's my perfect dog, but it's not the right time for me to have one yet, so perhaps she'll be right for one of your readers."

"Ah, that's lovely," said Becky. "That will really encourage people to give her a home."

Leah saw how difficult Amy was finding it, and leaped in, talking about the benefits of choosing an older dog like Millie or Maeve over a puppy. Then, "I'll take you back to reception now," she told Becky

123

and Joe. "Sian wanted to talk to you about how readers can support the centre, not just by adopting a dog, but by giving food and supplies or a donation, or volunteering."

"Great, thanks, Leah," said Becky, "and thanks, Amy," she called, as they followed Leah back across the courtyard. When Leah glanced back, Amy gave her a grateful smile. Then she put her arms round Maeve and gave her a huge cuddle, as her tears splashed on to the dog's newly shiny coat.

CHAPTER NINE

"Wow, it's busy today!" said Leah, as she and Amy walked into the reception of the rescue centre the next morning. Someone staggered in behind them with a big bag of dog food they'd bought to donate to the centre, and there was a queue at the desk, which Amy soon realized was made up of people asking about becoming volunteers or adopting a dog. Sian and Alex were busy helping them and Jack was on the phone.

"Hi, girls," Sian called out. "Look what a difference your article has made!"

Leah and Amy stared at each other. They couldn't believe all this was down to them!

Jack put down the phone and came over. "We've had three enquiries about the new puppies already," he told them. "They won't be ready to leave Mabel yet, of course, but thanks to you, they'll have new homes to go to when they are. A lady has left her number for us to give her a call about Lucky when she's better, too, as she's

looking for a female Lab puppy to adopt right away. And someone's called up to ask about Mabel. She's coming in later today."

"Wow!" cried Amy, "and it's only just ten o'clock!" She was secretly relieved that Maeve hadn't been mentioned, but then she felt bad about that – if she couldn't give her a new home, then of course she wanted someone else to.

Just then, Sian called the girls over.

"Leah, this family would like to have a look at the new puppies," she said. "I wouldn't normally ask this, but we're so busy – could you take them down to meet them and answer any questions?"

Leah looked really pleased. "Of course," she said, beaming at the little boy who stood between his parents. "Follow me."

"And Amy," Sian continued, "sorry to be cheeky, but that lady has come to meet the older Labs." She gestured to a middle-aged woman sitting on one of the plastic chairs, reading a leaflet. "She'd like to adopt one right away, and Mabel won't be available until her puppies have gone, so that leaves Millie and Maeve. Could you show her to their pen, please?"

Amy forced herself to smile at the lady, who introduced herself as Joyce, and led her out to the courtyard kennels.

Maeve and Millie both came up to Amy

and Joyce immediately, tails wagging, for a fuss and cuddle. "Oh, they're both lovely," Joyce exclaimed.

"Shall we take them for a little walk," Amy asked, "to give you a chance to get to know them better?"

"Oh, that would be nice, dear," said Joyce, so Amy collected the dogs' leads from the peg outside their pen and clipped them on. She found herself handing Millie's lead to Joyce, and holding Maeve's herself.

As they walked slowly round the field, Joyce told her about losing her old dog, Piper, who'd been a yellow Lab, too. "I didn't think I'd ever want another dog after she died, but I really do miss the company," she said. "I feel too old to go running round after a puppy, but when I saw that these poor mother Labs were in need of homes, I took it as a sign. They're both gorgeous, aren't they? However will I choose between them?"

Amy wanted to shout out, "Choose Millie!" but she clamped her lips shut. She knew that wouldn't be fair on Maeve, who was just as deserving of a lovely new home with Joyce.

They got back to the courtyard and let Millie and Maeve into their pen, where they each had a drink and stretched out on the floor. "Thank you for showing them to me, dear," Joyce said to Amy. "I would definitely like to offer one of them a home.

I think it's best if I go and have a coffee and think about which one. I'll be back in half an hour."

"That's fine," said Amy, biting back her tears. She couldn't bear to think that she could soon be saying goodbye to Maeve. "See you then."

Just as Joyce headed off towards the reception, Leah burst into the courtyard from the walkway that led to Mabel and the puppies' pen. She was herding a family with two young girls in front of her. "I know you said you wanted a Labrador pup," she said to the girls' father, "but it's worth thinking about an older dog, a cross-breed, perhaps. If you just follow me down here, there are some lovely ones to choose from, and they're all in need of loving new homes. My Rufus—"

"But we really were looking for a puppy," the girls' mother said. "And I've had my heart set on a Lab since I was a girl."

"Yes, but once you see the lovely choice of older rescue dogs we have here, I'm sure—" Leah started to say.

Sian came into the courtyard then. She smiled at the girls' parents. "If you'd like to put yourself down for one of the puppies, that's fantastic," she told them warmly. "Just go and see Alex at reception and he'll sign you up. In a few weeks you can come and choose which one you'd like. You'll be able to see their different personalities much more by then."

"Thanks, we'll do that," said the girls' mother, and the family headed for the reception.

"Erm, Leah," said Sian, with a smile, "I know you mean well, and that it's harder to rehome the adult dogs, but we're very grateful that people who want a puppy are coming to us as well and not going to irresponsible breeders or puppy farms. There is the right dog for everyone, don't forget."

Leah shrugged. "I suppose," she mumbled.

"That first family you showed the puppies to – when they came back to reception to put themselves on the list for one, they told me that they were just going to reply to an ad in the paper before they saw your article," Sian said. "So you've already made a difference."

"Wow, Amy, isn't that amazing?" Leah gasped. "Our article really has helped!" She hugged her friend tight.

"Yes, it's great," said Amy, but she couldn't feel too excited. She was thinking about Joyce, and how she might choose Maeve. "Sian, do you mind if I bring Maeve into the courtyard for a brush-down, before Joyce comes back?" she asked.

"Yes, of course," said Sian, with a sympathetic smile that showed Amy she understood exactly how she was feeling.

"I'm going to miss you so much," Amy told Maeve a few minutes later, as she brushed her gently. "Even if Joyce doesn't choose you this morning, I know someone else will, and soon. And I'm happy for you, I really am. I just can't bear to think about letting you go." She gazed at Maeve and Maeve looked back at her, as if she understood that she and Amy couldn't be together forever, and was just as upset about it.

Just then, Amy heard footsteps behind her. She looked up, expecting to see Joyce, but it was…

"Mum! What are you doing here?" she cried.

"We're not too late, are we?" gasped Mum. She looked flustered, like she'd been hurrying, and she was holding a copy of the local paper in her hand.

Amy looked puzzled. "Too late for what?"

"To adopt Maeve," said Mum breathlessly. "Sian just told me there was someone else interested…"

Amy stared at Mum, her eyes wide with surprise. "What are you talking about?" she gasped. "I thought we couldn't…"

"I just read this," said Mum, waving the paper at her. "Your article. And it got me thinking. Seriously thinking. I've changed my mind. Maeve would be calmer and easier to handle than a puppy, and I know I'd have to walk her while you're at school in the week and when you're at your dad's, but getting outdoors would be good for me. I think this would be good for us. *She* could be good for us."

"Mum, what are you saying?" Amy cried.

"You said Maeve was your perfect dog," Mum said. "And when I met her, and saw you together, I guess I knew that, too – although I couldn't admit it to myself at the time. But when I saw the picture, in here, I just knew it. I knew you should be together."

"She is, she is my perfect dog," Amy cried, hugging Maeve fiercely.

"I'll go and talk to Alex right now," said Mum, and hurried off again.

Amy gave Maeve another hug and laughed out loud. "Did that really just happen?" she asked her. "I can't believe it! I'll be back soon, OK?" In a daze she put Maeve in her pen and hurried off to find Leah. She gabbled out the whole story of Mum turning up, and the article. When she said that Mum was talking to Alex about Maeve at that exact moment, Leah grabbed her hand and said, "What are you waiting for, then? Come on!" and virtually dragged her back to reception. The two girls burst through the door to find Mum deep in conversation with Alex and Sian.

"So, is it OK for us to have Maeve?" asked Amy.

"Well, I was right about the insurance

costs," Mum sighed, frowning. "And there are the guests to consider – Alex tells me that Labradors are notorious stealers of food…"

Amy's stomach flipped over. Was Mum changing her mind?

"It's not going to be easy," she heard her say, "but I can't imagine us *not* having her now. She's coming home with us."

"Oh, Mum, thanks!" Amy gasped, rushing to hug her. Then she hugged Leah for a long time, too, and when they broke apart she saw that Alex, Mum and Sian were all smiling at her.

Just then Joyce walked back in. "Hello!" she said brightly.

"Oh, Joyce, I'm afraid Maeve's reserved now … by Amy!" said Sian. "Millie's still available, though."

Joyce beamed at them. "Oh, that's wonderful news, dear," she said to Amy. "And it's helped me out. I still didn't know who to choose, and now my decision is made. Millie will make me a wonderful companion!"

"They'll both have new homes – brilliant!" cried Leah.

"And that lady's coming in this afternoon to see about Mabel, and the volunteer who's looking after the quarantined puppy wants to keep her," Sian told them. "I'm sure we'll soon find homes for Lucky and Scout and get families signed up for the rest of the new puppies in no time." She turned to Leah. "And what you said about

139

adopting a cross-breed in your article has worked wonders, too, because we've had three families booking in to come and meet our rescue dogs this weekend," she added.

Leah laughed with delight at that. "Yes!" she whooped. "Rufus will be so proud of me!"

They all went down with Joyce and Amy to see Millie and Maeve again. As soon as Alex opened the pen, Maeve came rushing up to Amy, with her tail wagging, and licked her hand. Amy gave her a big hug. "You're going to be my very own dog," she told her. "I'll take you for walks on the beach and buy you toys, and you can sleep on my bed—"

"Well, hang on a minute, I didn't say anything about sleeping on beds!" cried Mum, making them all laugh.

"Looks like Maeve's got her happy ending after all," said Alex.

"Well, that's another successful mission for Animal S.O.S.," Amy said to Leah, as she gave Maeve a pat, "and now we've got a new member of the team, too!"

Also Available:

A note from Kelly ...

Writing *The Hidden Puppy Rescue* was very special for me, as we have two lovely rescue dogs, Lottie and Finn. It was great to have the chance to promote rescuing a puppy or dog, and to alert readers to the terrible cruelties of puppy farming. You can read more about Lottie and Finn on my website at www.kellymckain.co.uk/animal-sos/dogsblog and you can find your local dog and cat (and even horse, goat and sheep!) rescue centres online, or visit national heroes, www.bluecross.org.uk, www.rspca.org.uk and www.dogstrust.org.uk. So, if you're thinking of getting a dog, think about a rescue!

To find out more about Kelly McKain, visit her website:

www.kellymckain.co.uk